Letting GO

Withdrawal

For Jonni Rhodes ... I'm a suspicious girl

First published in 2019 in Great Britain by
Barrington Stoke Ltd
18 Walker Street, Edinburgh, EH3 7LP

www.barringtonstoke.co.uk

Text © 2019 Cat Clarke

The moral right of Cat Clarke to be identified
as the author of this work has been asserted in accordance
with the Copyright, Designs and Patents Act, 1988

A CIP catalogue record for this book is available
from the British Library upon request

ISBN: 978-1-78112-838-1

Printed in China by Leo

Letting Go

CAT CLARKE

Barrington Stoke

Never make a promise at a funeral. It's my new motto. It's pretty specific as mottos go, I know. But I think it will serve me well. Next time, when someone makes me promise to help them scatter the ashes of a dead person, I will do no such thing. Maybe I'll say "Hmm" or "Maybe" or "Let's see how we feel about each other in a year's time. Maybe we won't even be friends then, let alone girlfriends." Yeah. That's what I'll do next time.

But this time I made the promise, and so I'm sitting in the back of an old Nissan Micra, listening to my ex-girlfriend Ellie's shiny new boyfriend, Steve, explain things to me. As experiences go, it falls somewhere on the unpleasantness scale between having all my teeth pulled out without anaesthetic and walking across a room full of Lego in bare feet. But this isn't about me. So I act like everything's fine. I'm really good at that. An expert.

Ellie keeps glancing in the rear-view mirror, and I'm ready with a smile for her every time. It's a constant source of amazement to me that a smile can convince anyone of anything.

I don't want Ellie to know how I'm feeling. I want her to think I'm the best ex-girlfriend in the entire history of ex-girlfriends. I want her to feel so bad about breaking up with me that she'll ... God, I don't know.

That makes it sound like I'm doing this for all the wrong reasons, but the truth is I believe you should keep your promises, if humanly possible. And this feels like it wasn't a promise I made only to Ellie. It feels like a promise I made to her mum, Janice, too. I liked Janice, and she liked me. She always said I was *good* for Ellie, and Ellie always pretended to be annoyed when really she was delighted. I was good for Ellie and she was good for me. When did that stop being true?

"All right back there, Aggie?" Steve says to me as he turns down the volume on his terrible, terrible music.

"It's Agnes," I say for the third time. "I'm fine. Thanks."

Steve reaches across the gearbox and rests his hand on Ellie's thigh. "We're glad you came today, you know," Steve says. "It means a lot – to both of us."

I stare at his big meaty hand sitting there on Ellie's thigh. *Claiming* her. Who the fuck does this guy think he is? As if he has *anything* to do with this. As if he would even *be* here if Ellie or I had a driver's licence. Or if we knew anything whatsoever about climbing mountains. That's what I keep telling myself, anyway. Because surely otherwise Ellie would never want someone she'd only known for a couple of months to be here today. Steve never even met Janice. He's nobody. He's a stranger. A stranger Ellie just happens to be sleeping with. And the thought of that ... well, it turns my stomach.

"Actually, could you turn up the air conditioning?" I ask.

"Sure thing," Steve says. Then he turns the music back up and starts tapping his fingers on the steering wheel in time to the music. At least his hand isn't on Ellie's thigh any more.

A few minutes later, Ellie leans forward in her seat and says, "I think that's it ... that mountain over there. I recognise it from the pictures."

I crane my neck to see. And there it is: Ben Venachar. It looks like any other mountain. Grey, craggy ... mountainy? Nothing special. But it was the first mountain Janice ever climbed. She told Ellie that it "spoke to her soul". I'm not entirely sure what that means, but I think it must be nice to feel that way about a place. I guess you need to leave the house to find somewhere like that.

11.56 a.m.

The car park at the foot of the mountain is empty apart from a beat-up VW campervan with the curtains closed in the back. Steve gets out of the car and stretches. His T-shirt rides up to reveal the trail of hair leading down from his belly button.

Ellie's been silent since she first spotted the mountain. It makes me feel bad for making this all about me. I need to be here for her. Then I can go back to my life of skiving off college, eating *all* the biscuits and lying on my bed listening to my most depressing playlists.

Steve's busy repacking his rucksack, and Ellie's staring at Ben Venachar, her arms crossed, eyes narrowed. At some point on the journey, the morning's blue skies must have turned grey. I didn't even notice. That happens a lot these days: me not noticing stuff. My tea getting cold before I remember to drink it. My mum talking to me for five solid minutes before I even hear a word.

Maybe I should give Ellie the T-shirt now, while Steve's distracted. But I don't want to make a thing of it, like it's some big statement. It's not. It's just me returning something that doesn't belong to me.

It's only a bloody T-shirt. So why can't I bring myself to do it?

It was Ellie's favourite. She wore it all the time, and every time she did, I would say something like, "Don't you think it would look so much better on me?" or, "If you really loved me, you'd give it to me." This went on for months until one day she took it off, stripping half naked in her living room, with her mum next door in the kitchen. Ellie handed it to me and I tried to give it back, but she wouldn't hear of it. She said she wanted me to have it. And then she told me she loved me. It was the best day of my life.

"You OK?" I ask Ellie.

She turns to me and tries to smile. "Yeah," Ellie says. "I'll be ... fine. I think maybe when this is done ... it'll be better." She looks down at her hiking boots. I think they might be her

6

mum's, but I don't want to ask. My boots are three years old and at least a size too small. Dad bought them when he decided that hiking would be the perfect father–daughter activity for the two of us. This is the first time I've worn them.

Ellie looks over her shoulder, but Steve is too busy adjusting the height of his walking poles to pay us any attention. The guy has *walking poles*, for fuck's sake. "He's … nice … when you get to know him," Ellie says. "He's a decent guy."

"OK," I say.

That makes Ellie smile – a real smile this time. "Maybe he's not quite your cup of tea," she adds. "But he's … he's good for me. Things are … simple."

I cough and turn away because I don't want her to see how much that hurt. *He's* good for her? Because things are *simple*? Steve is waving one of his poles around and making lightsaber sounds. I guess "simple" is the right word.

Ellie crouches down, and I watch as she checks and double-checks the box containing her mum's ashes. Then she carefully places the box in her rucksack.

We set off a few minutes later. Steve is in the lead, closely followed by Ellie, with me trailing behind. Steve walks too fast, and Ellie has to tell him to slow down several times before he gets the message. She's doing it for my benefit, because I can't keep up. I'm so out of shape it's not even funny.

I was never exactly skinny, but now I'm somewhere past plump and probably on the road to fat. I guess that's what happens when you hardly leave the house. It's what happens when you feel sad pretty much all the time and food is the only thing that makes you feel better. And the thing that drives my mum out of her freaking mind is that I don't care about any of it. I don't care that most of my clothes no longer fit. I don't care that my grandmother keeps emailing me articles about the latest stupid diets. I don't give a shit. And that drives people nuts. They can't understand it, because that stuff is *so* important to them. They can't get their heads around me being perfectly fine with how I look because *none of it matters*.

I try to distract myself from the effort of hiking by looking around. By being in the moment. Mum's always banging on about it –

meditating and shit. I try not to listen, but some of it must have seeped into my brain. The scenery is nice, if you like that sort of thing. A bit bleak for me. But I like the sheep. They're just roaming around, free as anything. How does the farmer keep track of them? I stop to take a video of some lambs frolicking. They're so cute I almost regret the lamb rogan josh I ate last night.

Steve stops at a fork in the trail and consults his map. Then he fiddles with the compass that hangs around his neck. "This way, ladies!" Steve says, and sets off on the left-hand trail. It looks ... steep.

He's got *all* the gear. Expensive boots, a hi-tech jacket tied around his waist. He explained that his trousers are specially designed to remove excess moisture from your skin. I guess his legs must be particularly sweaty. Ellie's wearing special walking trousers too, but I'm just in jeans. There was no way I could afford to buy special gear just for one day, and I have zero intention of doing something like this ever again. My thigh muscles feel like they're on fire. Mum would call it "feeling the burn".

It's been about half an hour since we passed the fork in the trail. Ellie slows down and says, "I thought there would be loads of other people here. Mum said it was getting a bit touristy on the mountain unless you took the ridge route."

"Which is *exactly* why we're taking the ridge route," Steve says with a smile, and I'm almost certain he thinks it's charming. (It's not.)

Ellie stops dead and I bump into her. "Um ... we talked about this," she says to Steve.

I can't see her face, but I would bet money that she's trying to send Steve signals with her eyes. Signals that mean: *There's no way Agnes can manage the ridge route.*

I clear my throat and ask, "This is the route your mum would have taken, right, Ellie?"

Ellie turns to look at me, and I manage to steady my breathing and look cheerful.

"I think it gets quite steep ..." she says.

"I can do this, El," I whisper. "I want to do this." I don't want Steve to hear. This is none of his business. "For Janice."

I can tell Ellie wants to argue, but something stops her. I think she likes the idea of following in her mother's footsteps, today of all days. And I do, too. It feels right.

2.17 p.m.

We demolish the sandwiches Ellie made in a few minutes. She handed me mine shyly. And that's when I realised she'd made coronation chicken, which is my favourite sandwich in the world. Steve sniffed his sandwich and wrinkled his nose while Ellie was rooting around in her rucksack for her water bottle. He saw me looking at him, so of course then he said, "Mmmm, this smells amazing."

I'm sitting on one rock, and Ellie and Steve are sitting on another. Their rock is a big flat slab. It looks more comfortable than mine. My bum is starting to get numb. A deep coldness has seeped into my body as we've been sitting. It must be the sweat, cooling and turning icy. Should have got some of that fancy gear after all. A pair of boots that fit at the very least. My feet are killing me. Pretty sure I've got blisters already.

The views are supposed to be spectacular from up here, but right now there's nothing much to see. If I squint a bit, I can just about make out the loch far below, but otherwise it's just ... grey. Greyness all around, whichever way I look. It's kind of depressing, but maybe it's right for today.

"How much further to the top?" I ask, then pop the last bite of sandwich into my mouth.

Ellie opens her mouth to speak, but Steve gets there first. "An hour?" He turns to look at the trail ahead, then he shrugs and adds, "Maybe an hour and a half, if—"

"So where's this sunshine you promised?" Ellie interrupts. "I thought it was supposed to be blue skies all the way."

Steve shrugs again. "You know what weather forecasts are like. Don't know why we even bother to check them."

"You did check it, though?" Ellie asks. "It's just I thought there would be a bunch of other climbers up here."

A flash of annoyance crosses Steve's face. "*Of course* I checked."

I guess it's left to me to be peacemaker, so I ask, "So, Steve, how did you get into climbing?"

"What's with all the questions?" he snaps at me.

Ellie must look as shocked as I do, because Steve catches her eye and looks guilty. "Sorry ..." Steve says. "I ... um ... I think we should maybe get going."

We set off again, and it's not fun any more. Not that it was fun before, but now it's even worse. There's no Steve chatter to distract me from the hiking. Or from the fact that this is bloody hard work. The ridge route is exactly what it sounds like: it's a fucking *ridge*. There's no path – just rocky, uneven ground. And on each side of that rocky, uneven ground, there's ... nothing. The slopes aren't really steep. But you just know that if you fell, you wouldn't stop falling till you reached the bottom. Or you might hit one of the small scrubby trees that cling to the mountainside. And that would *hurt*.

Every few minutes, Ellie stops and waits for me to catch up. I wish she wouldn't. And yet I'm glad she does. See? It's confusing as hell.

I focus on each step. Putting one foot in front of the other, over and over again. I try to ignore the sound of my laboured breathing. It gets easier to ignore as the wind picks up, but of course the wind makes everything else harder. It's the sort of wind you wouldn't really notice if you were walking along the street. It would just feel like a light breeze. But up here it feels vicious. Its icy fingers find their way into every gap in my clothing. They tug and claw at my jacket, trying to push me off balance.

This will be over soon, I remind myself. I'll be home in a matter of hours, back in my room with the door locked and my headphones over my ears. I hold on to that thought. I think about being wrapped up in my duvet. Snug as a bug in a rug.

It starts to rain.

3.40 p.m.

The clouds have turned gun-metal grey and are spewing angry, relentless rain. Merciless rain. My jeans are soaked through and sticking to my legs.

The wind drives the rain across my face, blinding me for a split second. I lose my footing. I stumble to the left but manage to regain my balance. My heart thumps so hard I think I'd be able to hear it if the rain and wind weren't so loud. It's the last straw.

"Ellie!" I call, but the wind whips my voice away, so I have to scramble to catch up with her. "Ellie! We need to stop!"

She turns towards me and I realise she's breathing almost as hard as I am. She cups her hands around her mouth and shouts to Steve, who trudges back towards us.

Steve's hood is pulled tight over his head. His face is grim. All traces of annoying easy-going Steve have gone.

"What's up?" he asks.

I look to Ellie, but she's not looking at me. I guess I have to be the one to say it: "I think we should turn back."

Ellie looks horrified. "What? No!" she says. "We're nearly there!"

I look to Steve for back-up, but he's busy staring at his muddy boots, so I turn back to Ellie and say, "El, come on, the weather's not getting any better. This is getting pretty dangerous."

Ellie sighs. "Aw, it's just a bit of rain."

"Maybe there's a reason no one else is up here today," I say. A thought occurs to me. A horrible nauseating thought. "Steve? You definitely checked the weather this morning, didn't you?"

"Of course I ..." Steve starts, then looks from me to Ellie and back again. Then he winces, and I know I'm not going to like what he says next. "My ... um ... my dad said the forecast looked fine."

I laugh, but there's no humour in it. "This is a joke, right?" I ask. "This *has* to be a joke. You didn't even bother to check?"

Ellie is staring at Steve as if she's seeing him for the first time. But she says nothing. There's just the sound of the wind. Roaring.

Then Steve mutters something, under his breath but I still hear it: "You could have checked too, you know." And the annoying – enraging – thing is that Steve's right. Bastard.

I open my mouth to tell him to fuck off, but Ellie gets there first. "I'm not turning back," she says. "I have to do this. *Today.*"

It would have been Janice's forty-fifth birthday today. I get it. Of course I do. Ellie made a promise to herself that she would do this thing on her mum's birthday, just like I made a promise to be with her when she did it. But sometimes promises have to be broken.

"Ellie, your mum wouldn't want you taking any risks," I say. "You *know* that."

Wrong move. Her face transforms into an angry mask in an instant. "What would *you* know about risk?!" Ellie barks at me. "You're scared of your own fucking shadow."

It feels like a slap. I've never been slapped, but I can imagine the shock of it. The sharp sting.

Ellie sighs an exasperated sigh and says, "Look, you do whatever you want, but I'm getting to the top of this fucking mountain and saying goodbye to my mum." She turns to Steve. "Are you coming or not?"

Steve's face is a perfect portrait of misery. It would be funny if this weren't so awful. Because Steve is stuck, isn't he? He can't side with me over his girlfriend, and he can't look like a coward in front of her. But he clearly wants to turn back. Anyone in their right mind would want to turn back. (I ignore the tiny voice in my head – getting louder and louder – which says that anyone in their right mind would have turned back at least an hour ago.) Eventually, Steve makes his decision. "I'm coming."

I look around me, which is pointless because I can see precisely nothing. The cloud is all around us now. Or maybe it's mist or fog or ... I don't fucking know and I don't care. "How much further?" I ask, and Steve looks to Ellie for an answer.

"Fifteen, twenty minutes tops," Ellie says. "I remember Mum said the last bit is steep, but it's just a short scramble to the summit."

The voice in my head is screaming, *THIS IS A TERRIBLE IDEA!* But the wind is screaming nearly as loud, and I can't leave Ellie up here with idiot Steve. "OK then," I hear myself say. "Let's go."

Every drop of my concentration goes into finding the next safe place to put my foot. Steve's poles aren't looking so stupid now. I wish I had something to steady me. It might make me feel less like a baby giraffe taking its first steps on an ice rink.

I don't look up. I don't look ahead. All I see is my feet. The ground is soggy grass, sucking mud or slippery rock. I can't work out which I hate more. It's all terrible.

4.14 p.m.

Top of the world. That's how you're supposed to feel when you reach the summit of a mountain, right? Like you've achieved something. You have battled against Mother Nature and *won*. Well, I feel like shit.

I'm sweating and freezing cold at the same time, which doesn't seem fair. The rain has turned to sleet – like needles of ice stabbing at my face. I keep turning my back to the wind, only for the wind to then change direction too. It feels like a giant FUCK YOU.

The summit of Ben Venachar is not much to look at. Nothing here apart from a pile of stones. I watch as Ellie takes a small stone from her pocket and places it on the top of the pile.

Steve crouches on one side of the stone pile, trying to shelter from the wind. His cheeriness has washed away with the rain. I should be glad,

but strangely I'm not. His cheeriness was …
cheerful, I guess.

While Ellie's struggling with the clasps of her
rucksack, I trudge over to Steve, crouch down and
say, "Hey."

He looks up at me, suspicious. "Yeah?"

I whisper, "Is this the worst date you've ever
been on or what?"

He does this sort of snort. I *think* it's a laugh,
but it's hard to tell because he looks so unhappy.
"This … this isn't how I pictured today going,"
Steve says.

"Tell me about it."

4.21 p.m.

I stare at the box in Ellie's hands. It's about the same size as the one Dad brought back from the pet shop the day after my grandfather's funeral. Inside was a tiny ball of orange and white fur. A hamster. I named him Derek. Then I renamed him the next day. And the day after that. The hamster ended up being called Wizbit, for reasons I can't even remember. Wizbit was a good hamster until Dad sat on him and he died.

Ellie's clutching the box as hard as you'd expect someone to clutch a box containing their mother. My brain has trouble computing the fact that Janice is in that box. The woman who said she wanted me to treat her house like a home. The woman who bought a special mug for me to use whenever I came round. The woman who said she thought of me as family. *Family*. The woman who demanded Ellie and I "dance it out" whenever we dared to enter the kitchen when she was cooking. And the thing is, I don't dance.

Dancing is *not* a thing that I do. But I made an exception in Janice's kitchen. Somehow it felt OK to dance there, with Janice and with Ellie. It felt safe.

And now Janice is ashes. Dust. How can that be true? How is that fair?

I'm still pissed off with Ellie. I'm still hurt. She shouldn't have said those things about me, especially not in front of Steve. But my feelings can wait. I need to be here for her right now.

I clamber to my feet and go to her. "Do you want to ... do you want to say something?" I ask. "About your mum?"

Ellie looks up at me, and it's hard to tell where her tears end and the wetness from the rain begins. "I'm sorry," she says.

I'm not even sure what she's apologising for, but it doesn't matter. "It's OK," I tell her. "It's going to be OK."

Ellie stands up straighter and opens up the box. She looks to me for reassurance and I nod.

She turns away from me and holds out the box. She tips it up.

The nightmare thing I've been worrying about ever since the wind picked up doesn't happen. When Ellie tips up the box, a gust of wind doesn't blow the dust and ashes back into our faces. So I don't breathe the remains of Janice into my lungs. I don't choke on her.

It's as if the wind *knows*. Just for a moment, it's working with us instead of against us. Janice is whisked away into the sky. She's flying.

4.32 p.m.

"We need to get going … seriously," says Steve.

I swear I forgot he was here. For a few blissful peaceful moments, I forgot that Steve even existed. It was just Ellie and me, saying goodbye to her mum. The way it was supposed to be. Ellie and me, together.

"Shut up, Steve." And the funny thing is, these words don't come out of my mouth. They come out of Ellie's.

She might as well have punched Steve in the balls. His eyes sort of bug out of his head. It's kind of brilliant. But then I see the anger appear on his face. "Fuck you," Steve says.

"Fuck *you*!" Ellie spits, and lunges towards him.

She doesn't push him, even though I can tell she wants to. So Steve doesn't fall all Humpty-Dumpty down the mountain. I find myself holding my breath as they stare at each other. And I can't help it ... the sight of the two of them in full hiking gear, hoods up and glaring at each other, makes me laugh.

Steve's head snaps round towards me. And I laugh even more. What is *wrong* with me? Then Ellie starts to laugh, and I know that whatever is wrong with me must be wrong with her too.

Steve clenches his fists and shakes his head in disbelief. "Stupid ... stupid *bitches!*" he says. "I wonder how hard you'll be laughing when you have to find your own way home, huh?" He picks up his rucksack and a pole, then grabs the other pole that was leaning against Ellie's rucksack. He gives us one last disgusted look and then sets off down the mountain.

4.37 p.m.

Ellie says something, but her words are whipped away by the wind. I step closer and ask what she said.

"Did that ... did that really just happen?" Ellie replies. Her voice is a bit shaky.

"I think so," I say. "Unless this is all an elaborate dream ... in which case I'd like to wake up now, if that's all right with you?"

Ellie doesn't laugh, which is fine, because it wasn't very funny. She's too busy staring at the place where Steve disappeared from view. "Do you think that means I'm dumped?" Ellie asks. "I've never been dumped on top of a mountain before."

"You've never been dumped full stop."

"Walked right into that one, didn't I?"

"Speaking of walking ..." I say. "How about we get the fuck off this mountain and figure out how the hell we're going to get home without the help of Steve and his wonder poles?" My tone is light, but really I am worried. If Steve drives off without us, we're screwed. We're miles from the nearest town, and I don't have cash for a taxi. The last resort would be to call my mum. It would take her two and a half hours to get here, but she *would* come. And I would never, ever hear the end of it. Not just because I lied to her – I told her I was spending the day with my mate Jamila ... That wouldn't even be the worst of it. The real issue would be me being here with Ellie. Mum never understood what Ellie and I had. She never even bothered to try.

Ellie puts the box back in the rucksack and settles the rucksack on her back. She turns to take one last look at the pile of stones, and she almost smiles. Ellie whispers the words, so I don't hear them so much as see them in the movement of her lips: "Bye, Mum. Happy Birthday."

5.04 p.m.

I didn't think the weather could get any worse. I was wrong.

I can hardly see a thing. Just flashes of red rucksack reassuring me that Ellie's still there. The first part is the worst. We have to scramble down backwards, clinging to the rocks as the wind does its best to pull us from the mountain. My fingers are numb within seconds, but by some miracle they manage to cling on. A single thought repeats in my brain, over and over and over again until it loses all meaning: *This is the scariest thing I've ever done. This is the scariest thing I've ever done. This is the scariest—*

Then my right foot slips and I fall.

I start sliding down the side of the mountain.

It takes a couple of moments for me to realise what's happening. As soon as I do, I flatten myself out like a squished spider. My hands scrabble to grab onto something ...

anything … a rock. A rock juts out and my right hand reaches for it, my fingers digging into a crack. Then my left hand grasps a small scrubby bush and …

I stop falling. I cling to the side of the mountain and rest my forehead on the muddy earth. Breathe. Just breathe.

I stay like that for a few seconds, then a boot brushes my fingers. "Hey!" I shout.

Ellie's face appears above me, and she's grinning. "Get a move on!" she says.

I realise that she didn't even see me fall. She was too busy fighting her own battle with this bastard mountain. For some reason, that thought gives me courage. If Ellie didn't see it happen, did it really happen? Did I even fall? I mean, I know I *did*, but there's nothing to be done about it, is there? I have to keep going. So I start moving. Slower than before, more careful. But at least I'm moving.

I laugh out loud when I finally reach ground I can stand on. I'm giddy with relief. Ellie hunches over, her hands resting on her knees. I put my hand on her back. It makes me think of the time she was puking her guts out in the bathroom at a party. Ellie wanted me to leave her alone, said she didn't want me to see her like that. It was early on in our relationship, when we still worried about stuff like that. The puking incident was a turning point of sorts for us. Things were more real between us after that. I guess that's what happens when you see puke shooting out of someone's nose. I hadn't even realised that was possible.

Today, here, on the side of a mountain, I rub Ellie's back again. "Jesus, El, you take me to all the best places."

She looks up and laughs. Then she does something surprising. She pulls me into a fierce hug. She's breathing hard, and I must be too. Both of us shivering. I'm uncomfortable and exhausted and cold and wet and ever so slightly terrified, but here's the strange thing: I feel *alive*.

I feel everything. All of it. The good and the bad and everything in between. And I could cry with relief. Because the truth is, I haven't felt much of anything for the past few months.

People say depression is like a black cloud following you wherever you go, but it's not like that for me. For me, depression is a fog. A grey fog enveloping me, cutting me off from everyone and everything. The fog makes everything muffled, and when everything's muffled, nothing seems real. It's hard to care about things when nothing seems real. After a while, you get used to it. After a bit longer, it's sort of comforting. A blanket of numbness.

But the blanket is gone. Today has ripped it from me and torn it to shreds, leaving me exposed. Everything is real and *raw*. The fear, the cold, the girl in my arms. The girl who broke my heart.

Ellie pulls back and looks at me. "Hey, come on, please don't cry," she says, and brushes a damp lock of hair from my eyes. "I'm so sorry. I should never have asked you to come today … not after everything. It was … selfish."

I didn't even realise I was crying. But now I taste the salty tears on my lips, and I laugh. I grip Ellie's arms, and I'm filled with a sudden need to make her understand. "Are you kidding me?" I say. "I wouldn't have missed this for the world. This is the best fun I've had in ages!"

She looks at me like I've lost my mind, and in a way I have. Or maybe I've found it.

I look at her. I really properly look at her for the first time since we broke up. I *see* her. And Ellie sees me. It's always been that way. The feeling is hard to understand, let alone describe. That feeling of being *known*. That someone else knows what you're feeling at any given moment. They don't have to ask. It makes you feel like you could fly. It makes you feel invincible.

Ellie's gaze flickers towards my lips, and that's the permission I need. It's the moment I've dreamed about for six months. Sure, I never pictured it happening like this. In my dreams, we weren't exhausted and soaking. We weren't on a mountain. In my dreams, we were in her bedroom or on a deserted street or a moonlit bridge (yeah, not sure where I got that one from). In my dreams, we weren't wearing mismatched bulky hiking gear, and my hair wasn't plastered to my face.

Dreams don't come true. I know that now. But sometimes real life can be better than any dream.

I close my eyes and lean towards her lips—

"Oh my God!" Ellie shouts.

5.34 p.m.

Ellie pushes me to one side and hurries away from me. At first I think she's going to be sick. The thought of kissing me has literally made her want to puke. *Nice one, Agnes*, I tell myself. But when I hurry after her, I see what she's looking at. A walking pole.

Steve's walking pole.

We stare at it for a few seconds, then both speak at once.

"Maybe he felt bad and left it behind for you," I say.

Ellie says, "Oh shit," and then, when she processes what I said, "Do you think so? Yeah ... yeah, that's probably it ... right?"

I want to believe my own explanation. But if Steve was going to leave the pole behind for Ellie, he wouldn't have left it like this. He wouldn't have left it here. On the edge of a steep drop.

Time seems to slow, and all I can hear is a kind of roaring noise in my head. But it's not the wind. It's my blood, rushing. It's adrenaline. Panic.

I pick up the pole and use it to steady myself as I lean out over the edge.

My first feeling is relief, because I see nothing. But then I lean a bit further and my heart slams when I see movement, maybe five metres below. And then I hear a voice: "Help ... help me ... Oh shit, it hurts ..." The voice is faint, weaker than it should be.

I lean out as far as I can, ignoring the dizziness that washes over me. "Steve!" I shout. "Can you hear me?" There's no answer, so I try again: "STEVE!"

There's a pause, and all I can hear is the wind and Ellie's fast panicked breaths right next to me. But then, "Yes ... I'm ... I slipped," Steve says.

"Can you move at all?" I ask. "Are you injured?"

"My leg ... it's ... it's *fucked!*" Steve replies. "There's ... it's not ... I can see ... oh God, I think I can see the bone." There's a gagging sound from below and a soft moan from Ellie.

"OK, you need to stay calm, Steve," I say. "Can you do that?" I don't sound like myself. I sound calm, which is miraculous, because I'm *freaking out*. "Steve? I need you to stay calm!"

"You try staying calm when one of your bones is sticking out of your fucking leg!"

Oddly, this makes me feel better. Steve is pissed off. And pissed off is better than terrified.

Ellie's already got her phone out. Good. That's good. She's thinking clearly. She taps out the numbers on the screen. 9. 9. 9. I've never called 999 before. I nearly did it the time my great aunt started choking on a fish bone, but Dad surprised us all by using the Heimlich manoeuvre. The offending fish bone flew across the table and landed in Mum's wine glass.

Ellie holds the phone to her ear, and I take a moment to breathe. It's going to be fine. Someone will come. A helicopter, maybe? Steve will be taken to hospital, and Ellie and I will be taken somewhere warm and safe. And one day the two of us will be able to look back on this and laugh. Steve will have a great story to tell his mates. He can embellish it and make himself sound like a hero. I suppose he's earned the right to do that.

This will be over soon.

Ellie turns to me, and I see it in her eyes before she says the words. "There's ... there's no signal."

I'm crouched down and scrabbling around in my rucksack before she's finished speaking. My phone is stowed safely in the pocket next to my purse. My fingers struggle to grip the zipper – maybe from the cold or maybe it's my nerves.

I press my thumb to the button to unlock the phone, but my thumb must be too wet or too cold, because nothing happens. I punch in the passcode. Six digits. I used to use my birthday, back before I met Ellie. Now it's a different date: the day we first kissed. Stupid, really. It's even more stupid that I never got round to changing it since we broke up.

I punch in the numbers, refusing to believe what the screen is telling me. But my phone is telling the truth with those two words in the top left-hand corner of the screen.

NO SERVICE.

"This is all my fault," Ellie says. "It's all my fault ... What are we going to do? What are we going to do? What if ... Oh God, it's all my fault."

Ellie has been saying these words or some variation of them for the past five minutes. I can't hear myself think, but I can't tell her to shut up. She needs to get this out of her system.

"What network is Steve on?" I ask.

"What? *What ...?*" Ellie says, her eyes glassy.

"His phone. Is it the same network as yours?"

Ellie shakes her head as if a fly is buzzing round her face. "I don't ... I don't ... How should I know?"

I try to be patient and say, "The two of us are on the same network, right? If Steve's on a different one, there's a chance he might get coverage here. OK, here's what I need you to do.

I need you to keep trying your phone. We might just be in a black spot, so move around a bit. We just need one bar to connect to the emergency services."

Ellie clutches at my coat sleeve. "I don't want to leave you," she says.

"You're not leaving me. I'm not going anywhere. I just ... I need you to try, OK? Don't go far, and for Christ's sake watch where you're going. I can't be doing with you falling off the mountain too." I smile, and it seems to reassure her. "OK, El?"

"OK." She squeezes my arm and moves away.

I'm not holding out much hope. Our best hope, I think, would be to climb back up to the top. There has to be a better chance of getting a signal up there. But that's a guess, based on ... well, based on nothing, really. Anyway, we can't risk it. If anything, the conditions are even worse than they were when we started to make our way down.

I check that Ellie's OK. She's shuffling around and holding her phone up to the sky. At least it's stopping her from panicking.

I turn back to the edge and shout, "Steve? What phone network are you on?"

There's no answer. So I shout the question as loud as I can. Still no answer. I lie flat on the ground and peer over the edge, and even lying like this the vertigo hits me. What if I fall too? My brain knows it's not possible, but that doesn't seem to matter.

I can see Steve properly now. Lying on a rocky outcropping. His trousers are black, but I see something white just below his left knee. Bone.

"STEVE!" I shout. "Can you hear me?!"

His right arm moves slightly. It's hanging over the edge. His walking pole dangles from the strap around his wrist. Maybe it was just the wind buffeting the pole that made his arm move and he's actually unconscious.

One last try, and I give it all I've got. "STEEEEEVE!"

This time, I close my eyes to listen. I hear the wind. I hear Ellie trudging around behind me. I hear ... a whimper. A whimper isn't great, but it's better than silence.

"Steve?" I say. "Can you tell me what phone network you're on?" A giggle bubbles up inside me, but I manage to swallow it down. This is ridiculous. How did this happen? How did I end up stuck on the side of a mountain, shouting about mobile networks?

There's another whimper from Steve, followed by a shout of pain. And then, "It hurts ... Oh God ... it *hurts!*"

I shuffle back and rest my forehead on the ground for a second. I've been freezing cold for what feels like hours, but now I feel hot. I could happily stay like this, cooling my forehead on the rocky ground, but I can't do that. Of course I can't do that. I know what I have to do. The problem is that I really, really, really don't want to do it.

It's hard enough to force the words out of my mouth, let alone make them loud enough for Steve to hear.

"I'm coming down to you, OK?" I say. I close my eyes as a wave of nausea and fear hits me. "Just ... hang in there."

"Don't be so fucking stupid," Ellie says.
She's looking at me like I've just suggested
something ... well, something fucking stupid.

"Got any better suggestions?" I ask.

"Yes! We ... we *wait*."

"Wait for what?" I say. "Wait for who? No
one's coming, Ellie. No one knows we're up here.
You do realise that, don't you?"

"But ..." Ellie looks around hopelessly. And
her head snaps back in my direction. "My dad!"
she says. "Dad knows! He'll be expecting me
home soon. He'll ... he'll call someone ... won't
he?"

Hope flickers to life in my chest. Yes. *Of
course* Paul will call someone. Hell, he'll probably
get straight in his car and drive here. He'll come
stomping up this mountain and take one look at
us and say something weird like, "Well, this is

a bit of a pickle, isn't it?" Thank God Ellie was sensible enough to tell someone where we were going.

"But …" Ellie says, shaking her head, and my hope dies.

"But what?" I ask, even though I'm almost certain I'd rather not know.

"He's … um … he drinks."

"What do you mean?"

"Since Mum …" Ellie begins. "I mean, he's not like an alcoholic or anything. He just … it helps him. He hasn't written a word since Mum died."

Paul's a writer. He gave me a signed book for my birthday, so I felt I had to read it, sex scenes and all. It's weird, reading that sort of stuff written by your girlfriend's dad.

"So yeah …" Ellie continues. "He probably won't even notice I'm not there. He's normally pretty out of it by mid afternoon. Sorry. I should have thought … but sometimes I just want to forget that everything's different now. Everything's … terrible."

Ellie starts to cry, and I want to comfort her. I want to take her in my arms and tell her that everything *isn't* terrible. But in order to convince her, I would have to believe it.

I take hold of her arms and say, "Ellie. We don't have time for this. Steve needs help, OK?"

She nods. "I should ... it should be me. I'll go down to him."

"No chance," I say. "I need you to stay up here. I need you to stay safe."

Ellie's eyes flash with anger. "And what about what *I* need? Why are you suddenly the one making all the decisions? Last time I checked, you knew fuck all about climbing." Her anger turns into something else. It melts and softens, and I see something in her eyes. It's something I've wanted so badly for the past few months that it's almost impossible to believe that I'm seeing it now. "Agnes, if anything happened to you ..." Ellie says, "I would never forgive myself. You're ..."

But she can't quite bring herself to say whatever it is I am. So I fill in the blanks with words of my own. "I'm ... the only one who knows anything whatsoever about first aid?"

A half-day course. Five years ago. And I can't remember any of it. But it's better than nothing, right? It has to be.

6.25 p.m.

The rain has stopped, which is something to be grateful for, I guess. I shout down to Steve to tell him I'm coming. He doesn't tell me not to, or even thank me. He just tells me to hurry. To be fair to Steve, I'd probably be the same in his situation.

Once I muster up the courage to start climbing, it's actually not so bad. I mean, it's not exactly fun – I keep imagining a gust of wind coming at just the wrong moment, making me lose my footing. I imagine myself falling, landing on Steve, and the two of us plummeting down the mountain. At some point my head would hit a rock and smash open like a watermelon. There'd be brains and blood and gore everywhere.

While I climb, Ellie's lying on her stomach, leaning out over the edge and calling down advice to me. "No, not there! Move your left foot left a bit! That's it."

When I'm just over halfway down to Steve, I look up and Ellie gives me a thumbs up. "You're doing great," she says.

Just as she says the word "great", I reach for my next handhold but my fingers can't get a grip on the rock. That would be fine if my feet were securely planted on the ground, but of course they're not. Panic floods my veins. My right foot flails around for somewhere secure to place it, and my right hand does the same. The foot finds its place first. Or, rather, my toes do. Just a few centimetres jutting out from the face of the rock. My legs are shaking badly, and I'm struggling to breathe. I take another look up at Ellie, and she nods her encouragement. "Nearly there!" she says. I don't think she even realises how close I came to falling.

Steve's ledge is just about big enough for two, and I edge sideways a bit so I don't step on him. When my feet hit the ledge, my legs sort of give way and I slump down next to him.

"Fancy seeing you here!" I say, and my voice is croaky.

"Weird coincidence or what?" Steve says with a weak smile.

He looks terrible. Pale and sweaty. And that's before I even look at his leg.

I think he's at risk of going into shock. That rings a bell from my first-aid course. Trouble is, I can't remember much else. I think he needs to stay warm? Luckily, Ellie gave me her spare fleece. I take it out of my rucksack.

"I'm just going to put this over you, Steve," I say. "Keep you nice and warm, OK?" And then I remember something else. You're meant to loosen any clothing that might limit blood flow. "Don't go getting the wrong idea," I say as I unzip the top of his jacket and the fleece underneath.

"What are you ... what are you doing?" Steve says. "I'm freezing!"

"Don't worry about it, OK?" I say, because "Trying to stop you from dying" might freak him out a bit. One of the most important things you need to do with someone at risk of shock is calm them down, reassure them. The first-aid stuff is coming back to me now – not as fast as I'd like, but better late than never. It's as if the information from the course has lain dormant in my brain for years, just waiting to be summoned when I need it most.

I fumble at Steve's waist to unfasten the top couple of buttons of his jeans. "I thought … thought you were gay?" he says, and I reckon it has to be a good sign that he's able to joke.

"What can I say?" I reply. "One day in your company has turned me straight."

Shit. I should have looked at his leg first. I remember it now: stop the bleeding, *then* check for signs of shock. *Shit*.

I lean over to get a proper look. "Right, looks like you've had a little—" My words are cut off by rising vomit, but I manage to swallow it. First aid is one thing in theory, but in practice it's very different.

"It's bad, isn't it?" Steve asks shakily.

"Nah, not too bad at all," I say, and I even manage a smile.

It's bad. His leg is a mess. A shard of bone juts out just below his knee, and blood has soaked through his trousers. I need to stop the bleeding ASAP, and there's only one thing left in my rucksack that will do the job.

Ellie's favourite T-shirt. It didn't seem right that I should get to keep it, but now it looks like neither of us will end up with it.

"I'm going to tie this around your leg, OK?" I say to Steve. "To stop the bleeding."

"OK."

"It's probably ... Look, it's going to hurt like a total bastard. But I'll do it fast."

I roll up the T-shirt and slip it under Steve's leg. Just that tiny movement makes him grimace and swear under his breath.

"Ready?" I ask.

He nods. "Do it."

I tie a knot and apply pressure to the wound. It's hard to judge how tight to tie it. Not tight enough and the bleeding might continue, too tight and I could cut off his circulation.

Steve cries out in pain, and the sound is just horrible. Like nothing I've ever heard in real life before.

"Is everything OK?!" Ellie yells down.

"Just perfect!" Steve yells back. "FUCK!" Then he turns to me. "I really, really don't like you."

"I know."

"Are you done now?" he says. "Please tell me you're done."

"Not quite. Sorry." I need to secure his leg with a splint – to stop him moving it and causing more damage. "Can you hand me that pole?" I ask.

Steve looks at me, confusion on his face, but he passes me the pole anyway. He watches in silence as I lay the pole down the outside of his leg then secure it with my bootlaces. "Clever," he says, and I'm not even sure he's being sarcastic. Then he says thank you, and he's definitely not being sarcastic. I shrug it off and ask to look at his phone.

It's a struggle for Steve to get the phone out of the back pocket of his trousers. He hands it to me without looking.

I take one look at the phone and sigh. It looks like our amazing run of luck is continuing. The screen is smashed, and no matter how hard I press the buttons, it won't turn on.

7.15 p.m.

I call up to see how Ellie's doing, but she doesn't answer. She must be somewhere trying to get a phone signal. I thought she'd have given up by now.

"How are you feeling?" I ask Steve.

"Like I fell off a cliff," he says. And I wonder if maybe – just maybe – Steve could be someone I might actually *like*. He'd have to tone down the mansplaining, but he's kind of funny. Maybe. A little bit. Or perhaps my judgement's gone right out of the window.

Steve notices my smile and asks, "Want to know something funny?"

I nod.

"I've never been up a mountain in my life." He giggles then – a surprisingly high-pitched giggle.

"What?" I say. "Ellie said you—"

"I lied," Steve interrupts. "On the dating site. I wasn't getting any … No one was interested in me, so I changed my profile to say I was into outdoors stuff. Mountain biking, snowboarding … climbing. I never thought I'd actually have to do any of those things." He gestures to his jacket. "This stuff cost a fortune. Anyway, what I'm trying to say is … I'm sorry."

I say nothing. What I *want* to say is: "You fucking idiot. This is all your fault." But what good would it do? He already knows that. Anyway, is it really true? Is it *all* his fault? I should never have entrusted my safety to some random stranger.

"You're not going to tell her, are you?" Steve asks me. "I mean, you can. If you want. But I'd rather you …" He closes his eyes for a few seconds, and I wonder if he's in pain. When he opens them, he says something that shakes me to the core. "I'm pretty sure she still loves you."

8.36 p.m.

The sun is setting over the mountains to the west, and I don't think I've ever seen anything so beautiful. I can finally see the lochs below, but they're now pools of inky blackness.

Steve's been asleep for about an hour. I wasn't 100 per cent sure about letting him fall asleep, but he was looking so much better, and the bleeding had stopped. I shuffle over to check on him. His breathing is steady, and his colour is good. Sleeping like a baby. Every time he shifts a bit, I tense up. What if I'm not paying attention and he rolls over in his sleep and falls off the ledge? That would be a ridiculous way to die.

The wind has vanished. One minute it was raging in my ears, and then it was just gone. Silence. Relief. I thought about asking Ellie to try to get down the mountain to find help but decided against it. Too dangerous in the dark. I'd never forgive myself if something happened to her. She can go for help as soon as the sun comes up in the morning.

I lie back down. Might as well make myself comfortable if we're going to be here all night.

"You still there, Ellie?" I call up to her softly.

"No, I'm at fucking Disneyland," she replies.

I smile. It's the most Ellie thing she's said all day. "Are you warm enough?" I ask.

After a slight pause, she says, "I'm OK." She peers out over the edge above me. "Looks pretty cosy down there."

"Sure you don't mind me cuddling up to your boyfriend?"

"Is he going to be OK?" Ellie asks.

"I hope so. I've done what I can."

"You've been ... you've been amazing." There's just enough light for me to see her smile. And just enough light for me to see her smile slip. "This is all my fault," she says, her voice thick with tears.

"It's not!" I say, and look over at Steve. Poor misguided Steve. He made a mistake – *several* mistakes. But he's paying for them now. "Ellie, this is no one's fault. Sometimes bad things just ... happen."

That last bit is true, at least. Bad things happen all the time. Sometimes your girlfriend's mother dies and your girlfriend dumps you and you just ... stop. You stop talking to people. You stop leaving your room. You stop going to college. You retreat so far into yourself that it seems impossible to find your way out. But that's OK, because you don't *want* to find a way out. There's no point, without the girl you love.

9.47 p.m.

Steve's snoring now. Snoring away as if he's snug in his own bed. Lucky bastard. Ellie's sleeping too – at least, she said she was going to try.

I curl up tight, with my hands tucked into my armpits. I try to think of warm things. Hot buttered toast. My favourite hoodie. That time I got so badly sunburned Mum said she could warm her hands on my face. Ellie's lips the first time we kissed. Every time we kissed. The last time we kissed.

I keep thinking about what Steve said. *I'm pretty sure she still loves you.* It's everything I've hoped for and wished for and dreamed about for the last six months. And yet ... I don't know.

My grandfather used to say that everything happens for a reason. He said it whenever anything bad happened. I think it made him feel better. Even when I was young and didn't really understand what it meant, I was suspicious. But what if Grandpa was right, and there's a reason for all of this? A reason for Steve bullshitting about mountain climbing. The awful weather and none of us bothering to check the forecast. Even Steve falling and breaking his leg. If none of these things had happened, I wouldn't know that Ellie still loves me.

Ellie still loves me. And suddenly I don't know quite how to feel about that.

10.45 p.m.

"It's so beautiful," I say.

My words are quiet, and I think they've been swallowed up by the darkness. But then Ellie says, "It is." I look up, but I can't see her. Maybe it's better this way.

I've never seen so many stars in my life. The view doesn't look real, which is appropriate, since all of this feels like a dream. The sky above looks like one of those photos you see on the internet, where you just know the photographer has messed around with the image to make it more impressive. But now I feel bad for always assuming that, because maybe those photos weren't doctored after all. Maybe the problem was me, assuming the worst. Just like always.

"Your mum was right," I say to Ellie. "This place … it's special."

There's a pause, and when Ellie speaks I can hear the smile in her voice: "I'm not sure Steve would agree with you. But yeah, I can see why she loved it so much."

"She was ... I liked her a lot."

"She liked you," Ellie says.

"Sometimes I used to imagine that I was part of your family," I tell Ellie. "I imagined those big Sunday dinners and barbecues and in-jokes were something I'd grown up with. Because I was always made to feel so welcome, right from the start. And that was down to your mum. I never ... I never got to thank her for that."

There's silence above me, and I think I shouldn't have said that. Shouldn't be bringing up all those memories. I'm about to apologise when Ellie says, "She would have been so angry with me."

I struggle into a sitting position. My limbs aren't working so well. They feel heavy, and there's a time lag between my brain telling them to move and them actually moving. "You've done what she asked, El," I say. "She wouldn't be angry."

"I'm not talking about that. She would have been angry with me for breaking up with you. She'd have been furious. I can hear her, sometimes. The exact words she'd say in the exact way she would say them. But recently I ... I can't seem to remember Mum's voice. I don't have any of her old voicemail messages. There's old videos, I guess. From family weddings and stuff like that. But I shouldn't have to watch a video to remember what her voice sounds like ... should I?"

"I think that's normal, El." I have no idea if this is true, but it sounds about right.

"I shouldn't have done it," Ellie says. My heart jolts, and then she adds, "I shouldn't have broken up with you."

So there it is. I look up at the stars, trying to remember the name of one constellation at least, but my mind is blank. My brain is a black hole.

"Why did you do it?" I ask.

10.51 p.m.

I still have the message on my phone. I've lost count of how many times I've read it. *"I can't do this any more. I'm sorry."*

It was a month after Ellie's mum died, and my first thought was pure panic. I misunderstood Ellie's message completely, thinking she was talking about suicide. I picked up the phone and tried to call her, but she didn't answer. I tried four times, then gave up and typed a message of my own: *"I'm here for you, OK? We can get through this. Together. Talk to me. Please?"*

I stared at my phone for what felt like an age, and then finally Ellie's next message came through. *"I can't be with you any more. It's not working."* And those words hit me like a sledgehammer to my stomach.

I tried calling Ellie again, but of course she didn't answer. I messaged her over and over, begging her to talk to me. I turned up at her house, but no one ever came to the door. And then I just … stopped. I let the numbness and the nothingness consume me.

"Ellie?" I say now. "Why did you break up with me?"

I half expect her not to answer, but she does. "It … it seemed like a good idea at the time?" she says, sounding sheepish.

I laugh – so loud that Steve shifts in his sleep. "Wow," I reply.

"I was a mess, Agnes," Ellie explains. "You saw that. And I … I was trying to figure out how to live without Mum. I was looking after Dad, and my aunts were calling me all the time and crying … *always* crying. As if they missed her more than I did. It was … it was all too much. And you … you were so understanding. You were so kind to me … and I couldn't stand it."

I say nothing. It doesn't make sense.

Ellie continues, "Yeah, I know. It doesn't make sense now that I'm saying it out loud. I think … maybe I was punishing myself?"

"OK," I say.

I hear movement from above and see Ellie's head poking over the edge. I can't make out her facial expressions, but perhaps that's a good thing. "I was being a dick," she says, "and I messed up the only good thing in my life. I'm sorry. Look, I know this isn't the time or the place. It's *all* wrong. But ... I miss you. Every day I miss you."

My heart is pounding now. Is she really going to say it?

She clears her throat. "I didn't plan for any of this. Obviously, with Steve ... I feel terrible about what's happened. But this has all ... I don't want to waste another minute. I want to be with you."

She said it. She said the words. And it's nothing like how I imagined it would be.

"Agnes? Agnes!" Ellie shouts. "You're not asleep, are you?"

"I'm awake," I say.

"So ... what do you think? Is there any way you could ... I don't know ... give me a second chance? Give *us* a second chance? Earlier I thought you were going to ... I thought you wanted to kiss me. I'm not wrong, am I?"

No. She's not wrong.

The day Ellie told me she loved me was probably the best day of my life. I felt validated. She *saw* me. She accepted me. It felt miraculous. She said it first, too. That was important to me back then. She chose to say those three little words to me. And I chose to say them right back.

"Agnes?" Ellie calls. "You're kind of leaving me hanging here. Can we ... can we try again?"

For the first time in hours, I don't feel cold. I don't feel worried or scared or panicked. A sense of peace has wrapped itself around me like a blanket. I'm perched on a rocky ledge on the side of a mountain, but I feel like I'm home.

I open my mouth to speak.

"No," I say.

11.03 p.m.

It surprises me. That I say no instead of yes. But as soon as the word is out of my mouth, I know it's the right one.

If Ellie had asked me yesterday, or even this morning, the answer would have been different. I wouldn't have even let her finish asking the question before shouting YES. But things are different now. *I'm* different.

Ellie says nothing, but I know she heard me. I wait to feel guilty, but it doesn't happen. Maybe I'm a terrible person not to give her a second chance, maybe not. I've spent the last few months of my life doing nothing. Mourning for Ellie as she mourned for her mother. I thought I needed Ellie. I thought I couldn't live without her. I was wrong. I can do things without her. I can climb fucking mountains if I want to. (I don't.)

There's a sniffing sound to my left, and I whip my head round. Steve. *Shit.*

I move closer to him, fitting myself into the gap between him and the mountainside. My body brushes up against Steve's in several different places. In any other situation, I'd be embarrassed.

I expect to see Steve crying, but his eyes are dry. He blinks slowly and starts shivering.

"How much did you hear?" I whisper.

"Enough," he says through chattering teeth.

"I'm sorry."

He sniffs again. "Not your fault. You're ... you're kind of a badass, aren't you?"

I laugh. No one has ever called me a badass before. I don't believe him. Not for one second. But maybe I *could* be one. Perhaps today could be the start of something for me. The start of me figuring out the kind of person I want to be.

"Steve?" I say.

"Yes?" he replies, and his teeth are chattering so hard now I worry they might shatter.

"We need to try to keep you warm, so I'm just going to ..." But instead of explaining any further, I just do it. I sort of drape myself across him, careful not to touch his leg. I put my arms around Steve and hold him tight. The weirdest thing is that it doesn't feel weird.

"Thank you," Steve whispers.

It takes a few minutes, but his teeth-chattering eventually stops and his breathing slows.

"I think I'm going to sleep again now," Steve says.

"You do that," I tell him. "I'll stay awake and make sure you don't fall off this stupid mountain."

Steve smiles. "Thank you." Then he grips my hand. "I mean it. I don't know what would have happened if you hadn't been here."

"Don't worry about it," I say. "You get some rest."

He squeezes my hand and then lets go.

Steve sleeps. I wait.

12.37 a.m.

I can't feel my legs. Or my hands. The numbness crept over my body so slowly I didn't even realise it was happening. I should probably be more worried about that, but I'm so very, very tired.

For the last twenty minutes, I've been calling for Ellie. Quietly, so I don't wake Steve. She hasn't answered. And I hope it's because she's upset and angry and hurt, even though I don't want her to be any of those things. I hope she's up there *hating* me. Because the alternative is too awful to think about. She must be so cold up there on her own.

I don't want to be with Ellie, but I still want her in my life. I still want to watch terrible movies with her and argue over the best pizza toppings, and I still want to be there for her when she needs me. I just don't want to be her girlfriend. I don't *need* to be her girlfriend. I think, for the first time ever, I'm OK with just being me. I realise I'm smiling and I don't even care how nuts that is. I'm ... happy.

A flash of blinding light comes out of nowhere. My first thought is total confusion. My mind can't make sense of anything other than darkness. My second thought is that I'm dying. And that makes me fucking furious.

A gruff voice starts shouting, but I can't understand the words any more than I can understand the light.

"Miss! Miss!" the voice shouts. "Are you OK?"

Ms, I think. *Don't call me Miss.*

I hear Ellie's voice. She's crying. *Sobbing.*

Then there's the crackle of a radio and the voice again: "We've got them ... Yup, all three. Just checking on them now." A loud, piercing whistle is followed by a shout. "Over here! We've found them!"

They've found us.

Steve wakes up, confused, and I tell him that help is here. He bursts into tears and says, "Thank God. Thank God," over and over again.

They've found us.

Ellie's dad must have raised the alarm after all. Maybe today he decided *not* to have a drink because he wanted to be sober when his daughter returned from scattering his wife's ashes.

They've found us.

Someone calls down to us, asking Steve about his leg. He answers the questions through his tears.

A couple of minutes later, a woman starts climbing down towards the ledge.

They've found us.

I've found me.

All I had to do was climb a mountain. And learn to let go.

Our books are tested
for children and young people by
children and young people.

Thanks to everyone who consulted on
a manuscript for their time and effort in
helping us to make our books better
for our readers.